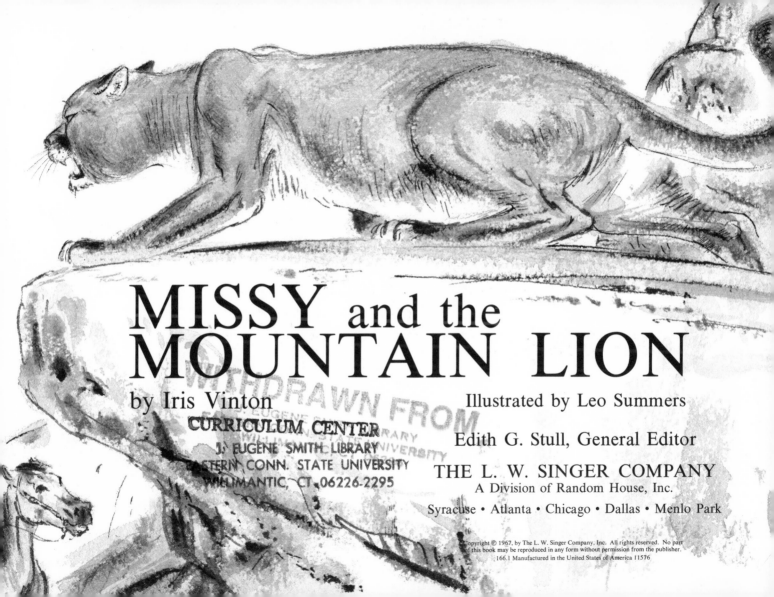

MISSY and the MOUNTAIN LION

by Iris Vinton

Illustrated by Leo Summers

Edith G. Stull, General Editor

THE L. W. SINGER COMPANY
A Division of Random House, Inc.

Syracuse • Atlanta • Chicago • Dallas • Menlo Park

2

That night Old Saltador,
the mountain lion, was hiding
in a tree.

He was watching for something
to eat.

3

He saw a calf come to the river alone.
He saw the calf begin to drink.
Then he sprang.

Leo Robson and his father
and the cowboys came to the tree
by the river.

They saw the marks
the mountain lion made
when he dragged the calf away.

They saw his paw prints, too.

"We must catch that lion
before he kills another calf!"
Leo's father said.

"We must catch him this time," Ben
said.

"No calf is safe with that lion around."

8

Leo began to run.

"What's your hurry?" asked his father.

"I'm going to get Missy," Leo said.

"You are too little to go
on a lion hunt," his father said.

"Aw, let him go with us, Mr. Robson,"
Domingo said.

Leo's father nodded.
"All right, then.
He can come along,
but he must not get in the way."

"I won't get in the way," Leo said.
He ran to get Missy.

9

Missy looked at Leo.
Leo patted her.

"You remember Old Saltador,
the mountain lion, don't you?
He hurt you when he came to kill
a calf."

Missy put her soft nose
against Leo's arm.
Leo patted her again.

"Well, that old lion came again.
He took another calf."

"Missy, we are going to hunt
that mountain lion.
We are going with the men," Leo said.

"Keep to the rear, Son,"
Leo's father said.

"Yes, sir," Leo said.

Then Leo, his father, and the cowboys
rode off along the river bank.

They looked for the lion's paw prints
in the mud.
They saw prints all along the way.
The paw prints led into the river.
Mr. Robson turned.

"The lion is on his way
to the mountains again.
Shall we go after him?"

"It will take a long time to find him,"
Jack said.

"He isn't far away," Domingo said.
"Look at his paw prints in the mud.
They have very little water in them."

Leo and Missy stopped.
Missy tossed her head.
She sniffed.

"She smells the mountain lion,"
Leo said.

Missy looked at something in the river.

"Missy sees the lion!" Leo cried.

Missy jumped into the river and swam as fast as she could swim.

She swam after the mountain lion.

Leo heard his father call,
"Come back! Come back!"

But Leo could not turn Missy around.
They were almost across the river.

The lion jumped out of the water.
He began to climb the high cliff.
Missy jumped out of the water.
She began to climb the high cliff, too.
Leo held on.

Old Saltador was climbing
up, up, and up.

He was climbing to the very top
of the high cliff.

Missy was climbing after him.

Leo called, "Stop, Missy! Stop!"

Missy would not stop.

The lion jumped to the very top
of the high cliff.

Missy jumped to the top
of the high cliff, too.

They saw the lion a few feet away.
He was snarling.

The snarling mountain lion came toward Missy.

She screamed.

She stood up on her hind legs and beat the air with her feet.

Leo fell off Missy's back.

The lion was about to leap.

Leo jumped to his feet and yelled,
"Missy! Watch out, Missy!"

The mountain lion turned toward Leo.
Then Missy's feet hit the lion.
The lion jumped back quickly.

He jumped back over the cliff.
Down, down, down he fell.
Missy stood still.
She looked over the cliff at the lion.
Leo looked down, too.
Far, far below, the mountain lion
lay still.

"Missy, Old Saltador is dead,"
Leo said.
"He will never hurt us any more."